Walt Disney's
Donald Duck, TV Star!

Written by Mary Carey

A Golden Book • New York

Western Publishing Company, Inc., Racine, Wisconsin 53404

B C D E F G H I J K L M

Donald Duck liked
to watch TV.
He liked to watch
people sing.

He liked to watch
people dance.
He liked to watch
people act, too.

"I can do all
those things,"
said Donald.
"I can sing.

I can dance…
a little.
I can act, too.
I will be on TV!"

"Oh, Uncle Donald,"
said Huey.
"Getting on TV
is not easy.
Working in TV
is not easy."

"It would be easy
for me," said Donald.
"Easy as pie."

Just then Dewey ran in.
"Come and see!" he cried.
"The TV people are here!
They are making a show!"

"Where?" cried Donald.
Dewey pointed.
"There," he said.
"Near Town Hall."
"TV, here I come!"
cried Donald.

"Wait, Uncle Donald!"
cried Huey.
Huey ran after Donald.
Dewey ran after Huey.
Louie ran after Dewey.

Donald saw the TV man.
"Please," said Donald.
"Can I be on TV?
I can sing.
I can dance...
a little.
I can act, too."

"That is nice,"
said the TV man.
"But I need a
stunt driver.

Our stunt driver
just got sick."
"I can drive,"
said Donald.

"Uncle Donald," said Louie.
"You are not a stunt driver."
"Shh! It will be easy,"
said Donald.

The man showed Donald
a car.
"A race car!"
said Donald.
"I like race cars."

"Good," said the man.
"You can drive it
for me.
Put this on."

Donald got into the car.
"Do not do it,
Uncle Donald," said Huey.

"Why not?" said Donald.
"I will be on TV!
I will be a star."

"Go!" cried the TV man.
Donald started the car.
The car raced off.

The car raced down
the street.
It went very fast.
It went faster.
"Too fast!" cried Donald.

Away he went,
down the street!
The car sped on.

"Look out!" cried Donald.
The car raced through
the park.

The car raced to Town Hall.
It went very fast.
It went faster.

"Too fast!" cried Donald.
Away he went,
up the steps!
The car sped into
Town Hall.

The car raced down
the hall.
"No racing in here!"
cried the Mayor.

The car raced out
the back door.
The car raced down
the steps.

Around the block
went Donald.
And around...
and around
again.

"Stop!" cried the TV man.
"Slow down!"

"I wish I could!"
cried Donald.
"It is not so easy."
The car raced through
the park again.

The car raced to
the lake.
It went very fast.
It went faster.

"Too fast!" cried Donald.
Away he went,
into the lake!
The car stopped
at last.

That night Donald
watched TV.
He was on the news.
"I was on TV," he said.
"But I think I like
to watch better."
"Hurray," cried
Huey, Dewey, and Louie.